Lady Tremaine

Drizella

Fairy Godmother

Anastasia

The Baker

D0007234

Copyright 2002 Disney Enterprises, Inc.
All rights reserved.
Published by Scholastic Inc., 90 Old Sherman Turnpike,
Danbury, Connecticut 06816.

No part of this publication may be reproduced in whole or in part,
or stored in a retrieval system, or transmitted in any form
or by any means, electronic, mechanical, photocopying, or otherwise,
without written permission of the copyright holder.

SCHOLASTIC and associated logos are trademarks and/or registered trademarks
of Scholastic Inc.

For information regarding permission, write to:
Disney Licensed Publishing, 114 Fifth Avenue, New York, New York 10011

ISBN 0-7172-6731-8
Printed in the U.S.A.   First printing, November 2002

WALT DISNEY
PICTURES PRESENTS

CINDERELLA II
Dreams Come True
An Uncommon Romance

SCHOLASTIC INC.

New York   Toronto   London   Auckland   Sydney
Mexico City   New Delhi   Hong Kong   Buenos Aires

"Come on Gus-Gus. Faster!" urged Jaq.

"What's the hurry?" wondered Gus as he raced out of the mouse hole after his friend.

"Fairy Godmother's here!" Jaq explained. "She is reading the story of Cinderella to everyone in the library."

Gus and Jaq arrived at the library in time to hear the Fairy Godmother read, "Cinderella and the Prince lived happily ever after. The end!"

Gus was very disappointed to have missed the story. "Aw, maybe you could read another one?" he asked.

The Fairy Godmother shook her head. "I'm sorry, Gus. But that's the only Cinderella book there is."

Then Gus had an idea . . . .

"Maybe we could make another book," Gus suggested.

Most of the other mice cheered. But not Jaq. "No, no. Who would read a book made by mice?" worried the thin little mouse.

"Cinderella would love to read it," said the Fairy Godmother. Then she waved her magic wand.

Poof! A book cover and paper appeared.
The mice and birds set to work. They
decorated the cover and sewed the pages into
it with a needle and thread. But something
was still missing—the stories!

The mice knew some good stories. There was the one about Cinderella's first day in the castle. And another about the time Jaq was human for a day. They put these in the book. Last but not least . . .

"Why don't we tell the story of Anastasia falling in love?" Gus offered.

That surprised the Fairy Godmother. "Anastasia? Cinderella's stepsister? That Anastasia?"

"Yeah," the mice agreed. Then they told the Fairy Godmother the story of . . . *An Uncommon Romance*.

The story began with
Cinderella's stepsisters
Anastasia and Drizella fighting with
each other as usual.

"That's mine!" claimed Drizella, pulling at a
silk ribbon.

"No! It's mine!" insisted Anastasia.

They tugged and tugged at the ribbon
until—*rrrriiiiiippp*—it tore in half.

Drizella tossed it back to Anastasia.
"Oh, you're right. It *is* yours."

Just then Cinderella's Stepmother came
in. "Girls! Girls! Stop all this bickering
at once!" Lady Tremaine ordered.

"Cinderella's ball is tomorrow night, so pay attention!" their mother commanded. "Every noble bachelor in the kingdom will be there! To find a husband, you must make the most of this opportunity!"

Lady Tremaine continued, "A perfect appearance is how to catch a proper gentleman. We shall find you men of wealth and nobility."

Anastasia became excited. "Maybe a count!"

"Or a duke!" Drizella added. They both began
frantically putting on perfumes and powders.

Of course, Anastasia and Drizella needed new
gowns and new shoes for the ball. "The fancier the
better!" declared Lady Tremaine. So they set off for
the village market.

"Anastasia! What are you doing?" her mother scowled.

The young woman jerked her hand away and left.

Then, as she neared the bakery, the smell of baking bread drew her inside.

She found herself right in front of the Baker. Their eyes met. He smiled and offered her a fresh roll. Anastasia shyly accepted the gift.

Cinderella was passing by and saw all this through a window.

Suddenly Lady Tremaine stormed in and snatched the roll from Anastasia. "I think not. Everything in this shop is . . . inferior."

"You could build a house out of these bricks," Drizella added, tossing a roll aside.

Cinderella watched, unnoticed, as Lady Tremaine dragged Anastasia out of the shop and hissed, "You're not to say a word to that . . . shopkeeper. I forbid it!"

Cinderella explained to her friends, "I know that look! I think they're in love!"

Jaq looked at her, laughing. "Anastasia's in love? That's crazy, Cinderelly!"

But Cinderella knew better. "Anyone can fall in love!"

"Heh! Anyone but Anastasia," the mice giggled.

"She just needs some help," Cinderella said softly. "I had lots of help, too. Remember?"

Jaq and Gus certainly did. They had helped her to meet the Prince! They agreed to help Anastasia and the Baker. But how?

"I know! We'll lure them into the square," said Cinderella. Then she whispered the rest of her plan to her friends.

To carry out the plan, the bluebirds swooped down and snatched Anastasia's bonnet, carrying it out of her reach.

"Outta my way," Anastasia yelled as she clumsily chased the birds. She shoved her way through the stalls and carts, causing everything to tip and spill.

Gus and Jaq led the other mice into the bakery. The mice tried to get the Baker's attention, but nothing worked. The Baker just didn't notice them.

So Cinderella leaned
around the door and
whistled sharply!

The Baker whirled
around. "Mice!" he
shouted.

The Baker began
chasing the mice out of
his shop.

Meanwhile, the birds dropped Anastasia's bonnet in front of the bakery. Anastasia rushed over, picked it up, and jammed it on her head. As she turned to storm off she ran straight into the Baker!

But before the two could speak, Gus dashed between a horse's legs and spooked the horse.

The startled horse kicked
out in fright, accidentally
striking Anastasia. She
flew through the air, past
the startled Baker, and
landed . . .

. . . on some eggs! Anastasia
was a mess! She was so
embarrassed that she ran from
the bakery, crying.

Anastasia ran through the market. Everyone laughed at the young woman.

But Cinderella felt horrible! This wasn't how she had planned it at all.

Cinderella and her friends soon found Anastasia.
"I saw you in the Baker's shop," Cinderella said gently.
Anastasia groaned, "He must think I'm . . . ugh."
Cinderella shook her head. "He saw it was an
    accident! Don't give up so fast."

"I'll help you," Cinderella continued. "Come back to the castle, and we'll clean you up. Then we'll get you two together."

"But mother forbids it! She thinks he's beneath me," replied Anastasia.

Cinderella smiled. "I think she's wrong. The Baker's terrific. And you'll never go hungry!" she added.

Cinderella and Anastasia
returned to the castle.

Cinderella cleaned up her
stepsister's face. "There.
Good as new."

"Don't stop now! Mother
says that looks count for
everything!"

Cinderella
disagreed. "You
want to look your
best, but that isn't
the most important
thing."

"Yeah, what I
need is a whole
new look!" said
Anastasia, not
understanding
Cinderella's
words.

They got to work. Cinderella gave Anastasia a dress and necklace to wear.

Anastasia admired herself in the mirror. She couldn't believe it was her!

Cinderella then gave her some advice. "Just remember, you'll catch more flies with honey than with vinegar."

"Who'd want to catch flies?" wondered Anastasia. She obviously didn't understand Cinderella's message.

Cinderella patiently explained, "The best way to impress the Baker is to be nice. You could start with a smile."

But Anastasia even needed help smiling!

At last, Anastasia was ready to meet the Baker again.

"He'll never be able to resist," Cinderella promised.

Anastasia was still worried. "But Mother told me never to speak to the Baker again," she said.

Cinderella took her stepsister's hand. "Maybe it's time to stop following somebody else's orders . . . and start following your heart. Meet me in the market at noon tomorrow and we will walk to the bakery."

Anastasia was so excited. "I can hardly wait!"

The next morning, Anastasia needed an
excuse to go to the bakery. She snatched up all
the bread and threw it outside. Then she
hurried to the carriage, calling,
"Mother! I have to run to town!
We're out of bread!"

In the market, the Baker had bought a garland of flowers from the flower man.

Shortly afterwards, Anastasia bought an identical garland!

Cinderella joined her stepsister in the market. With a few encouraging words from Cinderella, Anastasia went off to see the Baker.

But as Anastasia neared the bakery, she saw the Baker holding a garland of flowers and talking to a pretty woman!
Anastasia's heart was broken!

Anastasia left before she could see the pretty
woman's husband walk out of the bakery!
   Instead, hurt and upset, Anastasia raced off, tossing
her own flowers away!

The Baker spotted
Anastasia and dashed off
after her. He had truly bought
the flower garland for her!

He searched the market,
but he couldn't find her
anywhere. Where could
she be?

Anastasia ran past Cinderella, crying! Cinderella tried to follow her, but a carriage crossed the street and blocked the path!

When it passed, Anastasia was nowhere to be seen!

The tired Baker sat down to rest. He didn't notice that a goat had begun to eat his garland until it was too late. The Baker was able to save only a single flower.

Just then the Baker heard someone sniffing. He turned and saw Anastasia!

"Don't look at me! I look horrible!" she cried, ready to run again.

But the Baker didn't think so at all. "Wait! Please! Don't run away!" He held out the single flower. Anastasia took it and smiled!

To the Baker, it was the most beautiful smile in the world.

Suddenly Drizella and Lady Tremaine pounced upon them. "Anastasia! You were forbidden to speak to this man!" Lady Tremaine said. Drizella snickered.

Her mother grabbed Anastasia's arm and said, "Come along!"

But Anastasia pulled her arm free and grabbed the Baker's hand. "No, Mother! You're wrong. He's sweet."

"She's wonderful," the Baker added, looking at Anastasia.

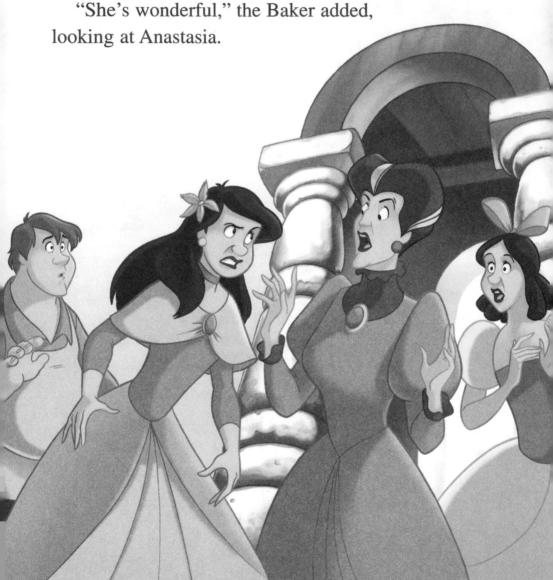

Anastasia looked at her astonished mother and stated, "We are going to the ball together!"

Lady Tremaine left in a huff, dragging Drizella with her.

The Baker took Anastasia's hand. Cinderella let out a sigh of relief.

So Anastasia and the Baker went to the ball.

As Cinderella and her Prince waltzed beside them, Anastasia whispered to Cinderella, "I'm so happy! I can't believe this! I'm so, I'm—I'm so—"

Cinderella smiled at her. "I know! Me too!" she said.

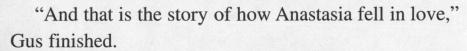

"And that is the story of how Anastasia fell in love," Gus finished.

"Perfect!" cried Jaq, closing the book.

The Fairy Godmother smiled proudly.

The mice scurried out to give Cinderella her gift.

Cinderella loved the book her friends had made.
Soon they were all sitting together in the library.
    The mice listened eagerly as Cinderella read,
"Once upon a time, there was a big castle . . ."

Cinderella was also on her way to the market. The princess had slipped out of the castle wearing an old dress so that no one would notice her.

But that didn't fool her friends the birds and the mice. "Morning, Cinderelly!" they called when they spotted her.

Cinderella put her finger to her lips to hush them. "I want to surprise the Prince with a garland of flowers," she explained.

She invited her friends to come along. So Jaq and Gus hopped into her basket.

Anastasia, Drizella, and their mother arrived in the Market Square. Anastasia watched as the flower man sold a garland of flowers to a young couple.

"Remember the tradition: give these to each other at the ball, and you'll always be together!" he said.

The flower man spotted Anastasia. "Need a garland of roses for the ball?"

Anastasia reached for the flowers.